P9-CEU-548

S'

"Help!" Yelled Maxwell

The Noodle Factory Children's Book Club Presents:

"Help!" Yelled Maxwell

by James and Edwina Stevenson
illustrated by James Stevenson

GREENWILLOW BOOKS
A Division of William Morrow & Company, Inc.
New York

Library of Congress Cataloging in Publication Data
Stevenson, James (date) "Help!" yelled Maxwell.
Summary: When a flood threatens the town,
Maxwell finds help in an unlikely place.
[1. Floods—Fiction. 2. Fantasy]
I. Stevenson, Edwina, joint author. II. Title.
PZ7.S84748Hd [Fic] 77-21247 ISBN 0-688-80133-1
ISBN 0-688-84133-3 lib. bdg.

1

All that week it had rained.

Every morning when Maxwell woke up the rain was *rat-tat-tat*-ing on the roof over his bed. On the way to the school bus he had to walk through deep puddles in the road, and his sneakers stayed wet all day. When he looked out the window of the third grade classroom, he could see rain slanting down on the playground. Water dripped from the seats of the swings and a steady stream poured off the bottom of the slide. Nobody was allowed to play outside. When Maxwell went to bed at night, the busy tapping on his roof was the last thing he heard before he went to sleep.

That was why he suddenly woke up. The rain had stopped.

Maxwell got out of bed. There was a full moon. It was warm and clear and very quiet.

"Hot dog," said Maxwell. Now they wouldn't have to stay inside at school, playing dumb basketball in the gym. Now he wouldn't have to wear his hot, heavy yellow raincoat. Now he could run around in the woods after school with Linda.

"Hey, Linda," said Maxwell. "Wake up." Linda, his black-and-white spotted dog, raised her head. "The rain's stopped," said Maxwell. Linda slowly got up from where she had been sleeping on the floor next to his bed. She walked over to the window and put her paws on the windowsill, looking out, sniffing.

"Isn't it great?" said Maxwell. "Let's go out." He put on his shirt and jeans and tiptoed past his parents' room and down the stairs. Linda followed, wagging her tail.

In the daytime, Maxwell could look down from

the front porch and see the rooftops of the whole village. Huxtable Falls wasn't very big. There used to be a factory with a small dam on the river near Maxwell's house, but the river was dry and the factory had closed down years ago. There wasn't even a waterfall now. The river was just a pond with skunk cabbages along the edge. The dam was high and dry.

"Come on, Linda," said Maxwell, running out into the warm puddles on the road. He kicked the water with his bare feet, and watched the spray catch the moonlight. Linda trotted after him, wagging her tail.

They went up the road past the last house toward the old factory and the bridge over the riverbed. He liked to stand on the bridge and see if he could throw pebbles as far as the pond. It was Maxwell's favorite place in the daytime. The woods were full of trees to climb and falling-down stone walls. There were grapevines to swing from, and honeysuckle and blueberries in the summertime. Linda liked

5

to disappear into the tangle and snuffle around.

Maxwell would walk across the top of the old dam. In the middle was a kind of door that used to go up and down in the old days, when they wanted to let the water through. It had metal chains and cranks to open it, but they were rusty now. Maxwell would jump down off the dam and make mud balls wrapped in skunk cabbage leaves, and throw them out into the pond. Splash, splash!

Ahead of him now, Linda suddenly began to bark.

"What's the matter, Lind?" called Maxwell. It was not like Linda to bark, except when the neighbor's yellow cat came by. Then she barked, and loudly, but the rest of the time she was pretty quiet.

Maxwell ran to Linda and patted her head. "What were you barking at?" asked Maxwell. Linda was standing very straight, her ears up, and her nose pointed toward the riverbed. Maxwell couldn't see anything. Linda ran on.

Then he heard the noise.

2

It sounded like thunder, or a train. Or a howling wind. Or all of them mixed together.

Just before they got to the bridge over the river, Linda stopped again and Maxwell almost tripped over her.

He could hardly believe what he saw.

The little pond and the mud and skunk cabbages were gone. Instead, there was a deep, rushing river. The water was roaring over the old dam and under the bridge, carrying small trees and branches. The noise was tremendous. As Maxwell stood staring, he felt water around his ankles.

"Linda!" he said. "It's a flood!"

They ran out onto the bridge and looked down.

Maxwell began to shiver. "It was all that rain," he said. "If the water gets any higher, Linda, you know what's going to happen? It's going to go down our street, and down the hill, and wash away the village!"

He turned and looked at the distant street lights in the village below, and he shivered harder. "We've got to do something, Linda—quick!"

Maxwell started to run back down the road, with Linda following. "I've got to wake up everybody," he thought. "I've got to call the police! I've got to—"

Maxwell felt like crying. "Help," he called, but he knew there was nobody around. "Help," he called anyway. Maybe he could run to the nearest house and warn them about the flood. No, it would take too long. What *could* he do?

There wasn't any time to spare. Some of the water was already creeping along the road. "Help . . . ," said Maxwell.

"What seems to be the trouble?" said a deep voice nearby.

"What?" said Maxwell. He looked around. There was nobody on the road.

"I said, what seems to be the trouble?" said the deep voice again. It was sort of a gurgly voice.

"*What?*" said Maxwell.

"I'm not going to ask you again," said the voice, rather cross now. "It was *you* who woke *me* up with your shouting and yelling and—"

Linda began to bark. She was crouching down, barking at a fire hydrant at the edge of the road.

"Keep your dog quiet, will you!" came the voice over the yapping.

"Linda!" called Maxwell. Linda stopped barking and started to growl instead. She went closer to the fire hydrant.

"Don't growl at *me*," said the voice. Linda jumped back, startled.

"Is somebody behind the fire hydrant?" said Maxwell.

"No," said the voice.

"Then . . . who's talking?" asked Maxwell.

"I am," said the fire hydrant.

"Fire hydrants don't talk," said Maxwell.

"Very well," said the fire hydrant. "If that's what

you think, then just hush up and leave me alone. As I said, I *was* trying to sleep. Good night and good-by!"

Maxwell and Linda stared at the fire hydrant. It was silent, and the only sound was the roaring of the river behind them. "I must have been dreaming," said Maxwell to himself. "Pretty soon I'll wake up at home in my bed. . . ." Then he felt water on his sneakers and he knew it was not a dream.

3

Maxwell didn't know what to do. How could he warn the town? If he had a pencil and paper, he could write a note and tuck it under Linda's collar—but he didn't have a pencil or a piece of paper, and, even if he did, Linda wouldn't know where to take the note. Maxwell looked at the fire hydrant again.

"Excuse me, sir," he said. "Mr. Hydrant?"

There was a low gargle from the fire hydrant. "What?" said the deep voice. "You again?"

"I'm sorry," said Maxwell. "But this is an emergency."

"Emergency?" said the hydrant. "Why didn't you say so? Emergencies are my specialty."

"The river is flooding," said Maxwell, "and if it gets any higher, the water is going to come down this road and into the valley and flood the town."

"Is that so?" said the hydrant. "What are you going to do about it?"

"I can't do anything," said Maxwell. "I'm just a little kid." He felt as if he might have to cry.

"So you're just going to stand there in the middle of the road, eh?" said the hydrant.

"What *should* I do?" asked Maxwell.

"Get help," said the hydrant.

"There's no time," said Maxwell, and then he did start to cry. But he swallowed a couple of times and stopped.

"I suppose you want *me* to take care of this," said the hydrant. "You want me to solve everything, while you stand there and blubber."

"You couldn't help anyway," said Maxwell.

"Oh, really?" said the hydrant. "So that's your attitude. . . ." He sounded mad. "I think I'll go back to sleep."

"Wait!" said Maxwell. "I didn't mean to hurt your feelings. I mean . . . *can* you help?"

"OF COURSE I CAN HELP!" shouted the hydrant.

"You can?" said Maxwell. "I didn't know that. I knew you helped put out fires and everything, but . . . I didn't even know you could talk."

"Typical," said the fire hydrant. "That's typical of people in this town. . . . I talk when there's something worth talking about."

"Will you help?" asked Maxwell. "I really need you. Will you?"

"Since you put it that way," said the hydrant, "certainly." He gave a wiggle, and suddenly he was wobbling into the middle of the road. "Now, you wait here, young man," he said. "There is no time to lose, so I'd better get started." He waddled away down the road. "Be brave!" he called. "Don't worry and don't cry! I'll be back before you know it!" Then the fire hydrant disappeared.

Linda and Maxwell stared at the road and the town below waiting, listening to the river.

4

"It's a lucky thing that Mr. Hydrant knows what to do," said Maxwell to Linda. "I couldn't handle this at all."

There wasn't much he *could* handle, Maxwell thought to himself. He could hardly remember the last time he had done something right. It was bad enough that he was the second shortest kid in the third grade—only Marcie Klopfer was shorter, and everybody called her "Tiny"—and when everybody had to stand in line according to height Maxwell was always next-to-last. But there were worse things. Maxwell thought about all the stuff he had lost over

the past few months. He had lost one model car (a Sting Ray) ; one baseball; a blue kite; a sneaker; two school books; his favorite baseball card (Thurman Munson) ; a bag of marbles; a book from the library;

the key to his strongbox; his jackknife; about six pencils; and a really nice ball-point pen. That was stuff that was lost *forever*. He wasn't counting all the things that were lost but he was pretty sure he was going to find again. Somebody was always asking him, "Maxwell, where's your ——?" and he was always saying, "Oh, it's around someplace." If he ever found all the things that were lost, there wouldn't be anyplace to put them. "You're absent-minded, Maxwell," his mother and father and his teachers kept saying.

Well, they were right. He was absent-minded. It was strange, but he just couldn't seem to pay attention to anything very long. When Mrs. McMillan, the homeroom teacher, started to explain something, Maxwell would try very hard to look at her, and listen, and understand. But, somehow, it didn't work. He could feel his mind beginning to slide away, slowly, from what she was saying. One by one, her words would begin not to mean anything, and then it all became a noise, going on and on, while Maxwell's mind went out the window, soaring away, here and there, until it landed on some other subject altogether. "Do you understand?" Mrs. McMillan would say. "Is that clear, Maxwell?"

"Oh, yes," Maxwell would say. "I think I've got it now."

Then she would trap him. "What was I talking about?" she would ask.

Maxwell would get red in the face and mumble, "I don't know," and everybody in the class would laugh. It was awful. Maybe he would grow taller someday—maybe—but it seemed as if he would never learn to pay attention. He'd just be a tall kid who couldn't remember anything.

When it came to doing things like chores or projects or homework, that wasn't much better. He could build a model car pretty well, if nobody was bothering him, but when it came to other things he didn't ever do them the way they were supposed to be done. If he was helping somebody with a project, the other person was always saying, "Don't do that, Maxwell!" or "That's not the way!" or "Not yet!" If there was a chance that something could get broken, then Maxwell was just the one to break it.

"Maxwell dropped my clay pot I just made!" "Maxwell knocked over the fish tank!" "Maxwell—the milk bottle!" There just didn't seem to be any connection between his mind and his hands. And that went for baseball, too. "Easy catch!" "Catch it, Maxwell!" The baseball would come down through the sky, and Maxwell would have his eye on it, and his glove ready, and it would be an easy out—then *thunk*. The baseball would be on the ground between his sneakers, and everybody would be yelling at him. That was awful, too. No wonder he was always picked last.

"There really isn't one thing I can think of that I'm good at," said Maxwell to Linda. "That's why I'm so glad Mr. Hydrant is here. He'll save the town."

He looked down the road. Where *was* that hydrant, anyway? He should have been back by now.

5

Maxwell waited, trying to be brave and trying not to worry and trying not to cry, just the way the fire hydrant had said. Then he began to wonder if the fire hydrant would ever come back. Where had he gone? What was he doing? One thing was sure: the fire hydrant had left. Where he had stood before, at the side of the road, there was no hydrant now. Maxwell patted Linda and waited.

"I'll count to a hundred," said Maxwell to himself, "and maybe he'll come back before I finish." He wondered how fast he should count. Slowly, he decided.

". . . twenty-three . . . twenty-four . . . twenty—"

Linda suddenly barked. A light was moving toward them up the road. It was wavering back and forth, but it was getting nearer and nearer.

"Look, Linda," said Maxwell. "Do you see what I see?"

Linda barked louder.

Coming toward them was a street light—all lit up and twenty feet high. It was tilting this way and that as it came, and it was dragging some wires. "Hurry up, Larry," yelled a voice. "It's not much farther. Come on!" It was the fire hydrant, leading the way.

"I *am* hurrying," said the street light in a high, shrill voice. "Goodness, what a hill!"

"Well, hurry faster," said the hydrant, thumping along. "This is an emergency."

"It *better* be an emergency," said the street light. "I mean, there I was on my corner at Elm Street and Main, doing my job as always, keeping things light and bright and cheerful, and then you came running along—"

"Cut the blather, Larry!" ordered the hydrant.

26

"Now, here we are—here're the kid and the dog."

"Hello," said Maxwell.

"Everything okay so far?" asked the hydrant. "Any more water?"

"No, sir," said Maxwell. Now the road was all lit up by the street light.

"This is Larry from Main Street," said the hydrant. "He's going to give us some help."

Maxwell looked up into the brightness. "How do

you do?" he said. "I'm Maxwell, and this is my dog, Linda."

"I've seen you downtown," said the street light. "You have a blue bicycle, I believe."

"No time for chatter!" said the hydrant. "Follow me, Larry, and let's get some light on the river."

The hydrant and the street light moved on, and Maxwell and Linda were in the dark again.

In a few moments they saw the light coming back and heard the hydrant talking. "It looks plenty serious," the hydrant was saying. "We're going to have to pile some dirt along the edge of the river to block off the road before the water gets any higher."

"Don't ask me about floods," said the street light. "I don't know the first thing about floods. I've never even seen a flood. All I know is street corners."

"Be quiet, Larry," said the hydrant. "I have to think."

The hydrant stood still in the middle of the road, casting a long shadow from the light.

29

The street light spoke to Maxwell quietly while the hydrant was thinking. "Sometimes I've seen you take the corner on your bicycle at high speed," he said. "That's very dangerous, you know. You should always stop at—"

"Pipe down!" yelled the hydrant. "Okay. I've got a plan. I have to go get things organized, then I'll be back. You wait here, Larry, with Maxwell and Linda."

"That's fine with me," said Larry. "I'm still pooped from climbing that hill."

"I'll be back soon!" called the hydrant, and he went down the road to town once more.

6

"Nice woods you have around here," said Larry, lighting up the trees. "Very scenic. I never get to the country. It must be lovely in the autumn."

"It is," said Maxwell. He was trying to listen to the river, but the street light wouldn't stop talking.

"All the leaves turning red and yellow and orange," said Larry. "Gorgeous. The sharp smell of apples and—it is apples, isn't it? That's what I've heard. Or is it pumpkins?"

"It depends," said Maxwell.

Suddenly there was a clanking, clattering noise from down the road.

"Now who's that?" said Larry. He turned his light

31

toward the sound. "Oh, for heaven's sake," he said in a disgusted voice. "It's those stupid gas pumps from Al's Service Station."

Maxwell looked. Sure enough, two gas pumps—one yellow and one red—were coming toward them, banging into each other as they hurried along.

"Hey, hey, hey!" shouted the red pump. "Where's the disaster?"

"Has the flood started yet?" yelled the yellow pump. They crashed into each other again. "Watch it, High Test," said the yellow pump.

"*You* watch it, Regular," replied the red one. "Oh, here's Larry!"

"Hey, Larry!" cried the red pump. "How's the old bulb holding out?"

"I'm fine," said Larry irritably.

"You seem to be a little dimmer than usual," said the red pump.

"Well, I'm not," said Larry.

"Just kidding, pal," said the red pump. "Who's this?" he asked, looking at Maxwell.

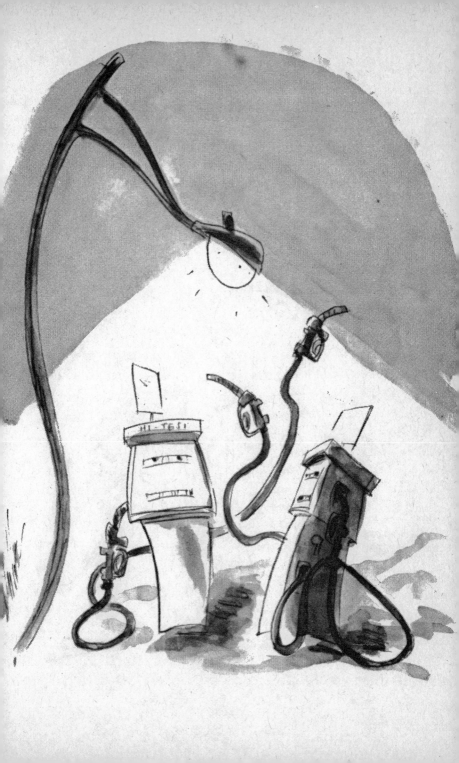

Larry introduced the pumps to Maxwell and Linda. "This is High Test, and this is Regular," he said.

"How do you do?" said Maxwell.

"Pleasure to meet you," said Regular.

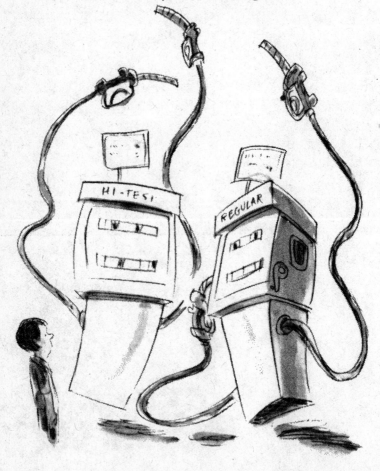

"Glad to see you," said High Test. He took a deep breath. "Fresh air," he said. "You can't beat it." He banged the nozzle of his hose against his chest. It made a hollow sound.

"No oil or gas fumes around here," agreed Regular. "Terrific." He rang his bell: *ding-ding-ding*.

"Where is everybody?" asked High Test. "The word in town is there's going to be a big flood."

"Everybody's coming up here," said Regular. "Harold Hydrant is in charge."

"I want to see the river!" said High Test.

"Me, too!" said Regular.

They both started running and crashed into each other. Regular went down with a terrific clatter, and High Test fell over and rolled to the side of the road.

"Clumsy!" shouted High Test.

"Me?" yelled Regular. "You're the clumsy one!"

"I think you broke my meter," said High Test.

"Serves you right," replied Regular. "You think you're so special."

"I *am* special," said High Test. He rang his bell

a couple of times. *Ding-ding*. "Seems to be all right," he said. "No thanks to you."

"And what about me?" yelled Regular. "I've got dents all over me. Paint flaking off. I look like a mess!"

Larry interrupted. "Why don't you two just go back down to your old gas station? You're not going to be any use up here with your arguing and crashing around."

"Listen to *him*!" said Regular. "The minute he gets away from his street corner he turns into a big shot!"

"Yeah!" said High Test. "Why don't you turn off, Larry? You're getting in my eyes!" He hooted and squealed, and Regular joined in. They ran toward the river, banging and jangling.

"Dreadful pair," said Larry, watching them go. There was another crash, and the arguing began again.

"I hope Harold gets back soon," said Maxwell.

"Me, too," said Larry.

7

Maxwell was standing in the middle of the road, looking at the water lapping around his sneakers, when he heard yelling.

"Follow me! Don't crowd! Stay in line! Follow instructions!" It was Harold Hydrant, riding on a big yellow ditch-digger. "Listen carefully!" he shouted. "We can save the town if you pay strict attention!" Behind the ditch-digger was a noisy parade moving up the road: in front marched a telephone booth, followed by a big mailbox; then a couple of garbage cans and a stop sign; three shopping carts from the grocery store came rattling and jangling along, and behind them was a washing machine from the laundromat. A big plastic ice-cream cone from the roof of the Frostee King came next, and then—flashing lights of different colors and playing loud music—the jukebox from the Huxtable Bar & Grill. The ditch-digger stopped at the side of the road next to

Maxwell, and Harold shouted to the crowd, "Proceed toward the river, everybody! Maintain order! Don't push! Be quiet!" The parade went banging and crashing by. "I'll join you in a minute with final instructions!"

The jukebox stopped. "Is there anything you'd like to hear?" he asked Harold.

"I'd like to hear silence!" snapped Harold. "You keep marching just like the others!"

"Gee," said the jukebox, moving along, "I just thought you might like some music to save the town by. . . ." He followed the others.

"That's the kind of problem I have to deal with," said Harold. "Everybody thinks he's special. Nobody follows orders."

"What are the orders?" asked Maxwell.

"The first orders were to follow me," said Harold. "Those were the basic orders. Then the next orders were to get everybody in position at the river so that they can be prepared to receive the final orders."

"What are they?"

"We haven't come to them yet," said Harold. "We're still following the other orders. What's the matter with you? Can't you follow orders in order?"

"I get confused," said Maxwell.

"That's why *I'm* in charge," said Harold. "I order

orders orderly." He sounded very pleased with himself.

"I guess that's the only way to do it," said Maxwell.

"Right!" said Harold. "Well, no dawdling! Let's go!" The ditch-digger rolled away, with Harold standing on the seat.

"Boy," said Maxwell. "Harold sure knows what he's doing."

8

Maxwell and Linda walked along the road toward the river. Maxwell was in a hurry to see how the work was coming along. He could hear a lot of noise up ahead. "With Mr. Hydrant in charge," he said to Linda, "I'll bet it's practically done by now. He knows how to get things going."

A big dump truck roared by, racing toward the river, and behind it came a bulldozer, clanking along. "Look out, look out!" growled the bulldozer as Linda jumped out of the way. "We're working for Harold Hydrant—and there's no time to lose!"

"Boy," said Maxwell. "He's got everybody in town on the job." He walked faster. They could see light

up ahead and hear a lot of shouting. As Maxwell and
Linda came around the last turn in the road before
the river and the bridge, Maxwell suddenly stopped.
"Oh, my gosh," said Maxwell. "Look."

Linda stopped, too.

They stood and stared.

It was sort of hard to figure out what was happening. One street light was on the bridge, and two others were wandering around the edge of the river, turning this way and that, sometimes lighting up the treetops, sometimes lighting the river, sometimes turning away so that everything went dark. But in the moments of brightness, Maxwell could see quite a lot.

The first thing he saw was the big mailbox running back and forth on the bridge, its letters spilling out, and yelling, "No, no, no—you're doing it all wrong!"

A traffic light was running after the mailbox, flashing red, then green, then yellow, and shouting, "No, no—they're doing it *right*!"

A garbage can was jumping up and down, clanging its top, shrieking, "Hurry up! The water's rising! Hurry up!"

"Not so fast!" screamed the telephone booth, slamming its door open and shut and ringing steadily. "Not so fast!"

The jukebox was sitting under a tree, playing loudly.

The big bulldozer was pushing dirt into the woods, shoving great mounds of earth in among the trees and knocking over saplings. "Not *that* way!" howled a Maple Avenue street sign. "Toward the river, stupid!"

The bulldozer stopped. "Who are you calling 'stupid'?" it growled angrily. "I know what I'm doing. Moving dirt is my business, buddy. All *you* ever do is stand on a street corner!"

The two gas pumps, High Test and Regular, were throwing stones into the river and shrieking at the splashes. "Wheee!" they cried.

The dump truck went thundering up onto the bridge. He had a load of cinder blocks. "Where do these cinder blocks go?" yelled the dump truck.

"They go along the edge of the river!" shouted Harold Hydrant, trying to catch up with it.

"I can't hear you!" yelled the dump truck. "That darn juke box . . . !"

"He said something about the river," called the telephone booth.

"River?" said the dump truck. "Okay." He backed up to the railing and dumped the entire load of cinder blocks into the middle of the river. There was

a tremendous splash—the hydrant was soaked—and the blocks disappeared from sight.

"Not *in* the river!" cried Harold Hydrant. "*Along* the river!"

"Sorry, mac," said the dump truck. "You should be more clear." He shifted gears. "That's that," he said. And then he drove away.

9

"Gee," said Maxwell to Linda, "it doesn't look as if they're getting too much done."

The mailbox marched over. "That hydrant doesn't know what he's doing," he said. "I should be in charge."

"You?" said the phone booth, running up. "In charge? Ha! Why don't you just go pick up all those letters you spilled?"

"Mind your own business," snapped the mailbox. "Do *your* thing. . . . Like getting wrong numbers all the time, and not returning people's dimes—"

"Wait a minute," said the phone booth. "I happen

to be a very important part of this town. People turn to me in an emergency. I'm the first place they go."

"Maybe," said the mailbox. "If they're in a big, giddy rush. But for really serious matters, people always write a letter. They know that they can count on me. I deliver. I never throw a letter back at somebody and say, 'Sor-ree—the line is busy.'"

"I only do that when I have to," said the phone booth. "It's not my fault everybody is always on the telephone. Besides, it doesn't take *me* two weeks to deliver a phone call."

"You're both useless," said High Test, who had been listening. "People in trouble don't waste time with either of you. They jump in a car, go to the gas station, and say, 'Fill 'er up!'" He rang his bell: *ding-ding-ding.* "Then they're on their way!"

"Sure—right into a traffic jam," said the mailbox. "Then they sit there for three hours, bumper to bumper."

"Not when I'm around," declared the traffic light, stepping up. "I keep things moving right along. I decide when they should stop, go, or be cautious."

The big ice-cream cone from Frostee King had been leaning over, listening, and now he cut in. "I've never heard such drivel!" he exclaimed. "You're all turkeys—each and every one. The town would be better off without you. All you do is make

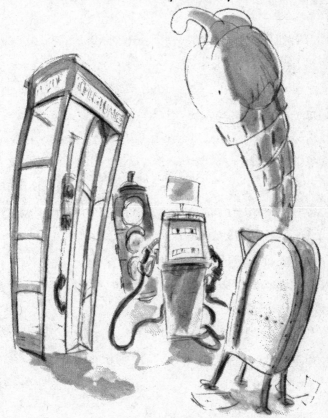

people miserable. You lose their letters and you give them wrong numbers, and as for that gas pump, you charge a fortune and you smell simply awful—"

"You can't insult me like that!" shrieked High Test.

"Who do you think you are?" cried the phone booth.

"You have some nerve!" shouted the mailbox.

The cone continued. "*I*'m the one that saves the day for everybody. Kids love me, and grownups, too. Dogs love me. Everybody does!"

"*I* don't!" shouted the mailbox.

"Go melt on a sidewalk!" yelled the traffic light.

"The fact is," said the ice-cream cone proudly, "when people's days have been ruined by the likes of you—they always turn to me. And I make them feel better."

"You make them fat is what you do," said High Test.

"I make them happy!" said the cone. "Have you ever heard anybody say, 'I'm so sad. . . . I think

I'll go buy a gallon of gas so I can cheer up'? Never!
But ice cream, good old ice cream—"

"*Music* is what cheers people up!" shouted the
jukebox.

Suddenly there was a crash from the woods. One
of the street lights had tripped over a log and fallen
down. "To heck with this!" he yelled. "I'm going
home."

"Me, too," said the bulldozer. "This place is too muddy. I could sink in it and never get out."

"Wait!" called Harold. "Wait!"

"We've waited long enough," said one of the shopping carts. "Come on, everybody." He rattled away, followed by the other shopping carts.

Maxwell walked onto the bridge where Harold was standing. "Is there anything I can do?" he asked.

"Do?" said Harold. "Anything. . . . Everything."

He looked around at all the things that were going wrong. "It's just too much for me," he said in a weary voice. "I don't know what to tell anybody to do."

"But if *you* don't know," said Maxwell, "who does?"

"Beats me," said the hydrant, and he started walking away slowly, wobbling from side to side. "I figured out all the orders except the last one."

"But the town's going to be flooded!" cried Maxwell.

"I know," said the hydrant. "I know. . . ." He walked away into the darkness. "I did my best," he said. "The best I could do." Then he was gone.

Maxwell looked at Linda. "I can't believe it," he said. "What are we going to do now?"

10

One by one, everybody left. They all rushed off saying they were tired, or busy, or it was too late at night. Then Maxwell and Linda were standing alone on the bridge, watching the water rush by below. A tree floated by.

"We're right back where we started, Linda," said Maxwell. "All by ourselves, and the whole town about to be flooded. . . ." In his entire life, Maxwell thought, he had never felt so helpless or so awful.

Over the noise of the river, Maxwell was suddenly aware of a very small sound. It was somewhere near him on the bridge. *Glup-glop . . . glop-glup. . . .*

"What's that noise, Linda?" asked Maxwell.

Linda was sniffing around, and then she stopped next to the railing of the bridge. "What is it, Linda?" called Maxwell.

He walked over and saw what Linda was sniffing at. It was a small brown oil can with a handle and a spout. It was lying on its side, making *glop-glup* noises and dripping little drops of oil.

"What are *you* doing?" asked Maxwell, bending over.

"I-I-I'm crying," said the oil can in a high voice. *Glop*. Another drop dripped.

"Crying?" said Maxwell. "Why?"

"I'm scared and I'm hurt," said the oil can. "I fell off the back of that big dump truck when he drove away so fast. He hit a bump and the next thing I knew I was lying here, with a bunch of new dents in me, and all alone. . . . I d-don't mean to cry, but I just don't see any reason why I sh-shouldn't."

"Oh, well, that's okay," said Maxwell. "I feel like crying myself." He swallowed hard a couple of times, though, to make sure he wouldn't. Linda nudged the little oil can with her nose so that it sat up.

"Thank you," said the oil can. Linda wagged her tail. "I feel better being right side up," said the oil can. "Tell me, why would somebody like *you* want to cry?"

"Because everything's awful," said Maxwell.

"Awful? For *you*?" said the oil can. "Are you kidding? I wish I was like you. I'd be on Easy Street."

"You would?" said Maxwell.

"Sure!" said the oil can. "I mean, you're big and tall—"

"*Tall*?" said Maxwell. "Me? I'm the second shortest kid in the third grade—"

"Darn right you're tall," said the oil can. "You're about ten oil cans high. That's *tall*."

"Oh," said Maxwell.

"—and you can run around wherever you want, as fast as you want, whenever you want. I never go anywhere, ever. It would take me about an hour to go to the end of this bridge."

59

"I'll give you a ride," said Maxwell, picking the oil can up by its handle. "You can go wherever we go."

"Thanks," said the oil can. "I appreciate that. My name's Lester."

"I'm Maxwell, and this is Linda," said Maxwell. He peered at Lester. "I don't see any really bad dents on you," he said. "A few scratches, mostly."

"Nothing serious?" said Lester. "Good. Anyway, I feel a lot better not being all alone."

"We're glad to have company, too," said Maxwell.

"Could you see if I still work?" asked Lester.

"Okay," said Maxwell. He pointed the spout at the road and squeezed his finger. *Glop-glop-glop.*

"Fit as a fiddle!" exclaimed Lester. "I wasn't sure, after that fall off the truck. . . . If I was broken, that would be the end. I mean, what would life be? All I ever do anyway is sit around and wait for somebody to need a little oil. They pick me up, point me at something, then *glop glop*—then they put me back in a pile of old rags somewhere, and that's *it*. If I didn't have my job to do, I'd be nothing."

"Well, you're useful," said Maxwell. "That's important."

"I guess so," said Lester. "I do my job. But I still wouldn't mind being tall and smart and able to run around like you."

"It's not so great most of the time," said Maxwell.

"I'll never believe that," said Lester. "You've got it made."

"And as for smart," said Maxwell, "you're the only one I know who thinks *that*."

"Of course you're smart," said Lester. "You got through the second grade, didn't you? I couldn't do that in a million years."

"I'm having some trouble with the third grade," said Maxwell. "My mind wanders."

"Well, put your mind on saving the town, why don't you?" said Lester. "That water is getting pretty high."

"I don't have any idea how to do it," said Maxwell. "I'm stumped."

"Well, with your brains you'll come up with an idea in a while," said Lester. "I'm sure of it. And if I can help in any way, count me in!"

11

Maxwell, carrying Lester, walked along the edge of the river, with Linda following behind. Trees and branches were being carried over the top of the dam, and some of the water was moving in a steady stream onto the road, while the rest of it raced on under the bridge. Maxwell tried to think, but his mind kept jumping from one thing to another. He could hear his homeroom teacher, Mrs. McMillan, saying, "Concentrate, Maxwell. Concentrate." That was about the last thing in the world he could do right now.

"The main problem is," Maxwell said aloud, "is—"

"The dam," said Lester. "You're right. That's the main problem."

"The dam?" said Maxwell.

"Right," said Lester. "It's blocking the water."

"That's what *I* think," said Maxwell.

"So what do we do?" asked Lester.

"There's only one thing *to* do," said Maxwell. "That's to . . . uh—"

"Get rid of the dam so all of the water will go straight down the river instead of onto the road," said Lester. "That's what I think, too. I agree with you, Maxwell, one hundred percent."

"Well, we think the same thing, at least," said Maxwell. "All we have to do is . . . is—"

"If we had the ditch-digger, we could dig a channel around the dam," said Lester, "and send the water through it."

"But we don't have the ditch-digger," said Maxwell.

"Good point!" said Lester. "You're right." He

paused. "Hey, does that dam open?" he asked.

"It used to," said Maxwell. "See those cranks and chains and stuff sticking up there? That's how they used to open and close the dam when the factory was working."

"Good idea, Maxwell!" cried Lester. "Boy, are you smart!"

"But it doesn't work any more," said Maxwell. "I've tried it when there wasn't any water around here. The cranks are all rusted." Maxwell shrugged. He was stumped. "So that's no use, unless . . . unless. . . ." He couldn't even think unless what.

Lester cut in again. "Unless I oil those rusty cranks and make them work again! Great idea, Maxwell!"

"How could you do that?" asked Maxwell. "There's a lot of water going over the dam. If we tried to walk out there, we'd get washed away."

"Okay," said Lester. "So what's the plan? Keep those ideas coming, Maxwell."

Maxwell gulped. He just couldn't think.

"Got it yet?" asked Lester.

"Not quite," said Maxwell. "Big ideas take longer than little ones."

"Excuse me, Maxwell," said Lester. "Could I throw in a little one while we're waiting?"

"Sure," said Maxwell. "What is it?"

"See those trees floating by?"

"Yep," said Maxwell.

"Notice how some of them bump into the machinery for opening the dam?"

"Yep," said Maxwell. "I see that."

"Well, picture this," said Lester. "If we were riding on one of those tree trunks, and steered it right, we'd be just where we wanted to be, wouldn't we?"

"I guess we would," said Maxwell.

"Then I could oil up that crank nice and oily, and you could turn the crank and open the dam, and—whoosh—the water would go through, and our troubles would be over."

"That's easier said than done," said Maxwell.

"What isn't?" asked Lester. "Come on, Maxwell—let's get started!"

12

Maxwell was scared. He was standing in the water up to his waist, watching for a good log to float by. This was the most dangerous idea he'd ever heard of. Linda was barking from the river bank.

"You've got a lot of courage, Maxwell," said Lester. "I wish I had your brains and nerve. And I wouldn't mind being tall like you, either."

For some reason, Lester's words made Maxwell feel sort of tall and smart and brave. But he knew he really wasn't. "I'm not any of those things, Lester," he said.

"And modest, too," said Lester. "What a great combination."

Maxwell didn't know what to say. If Lester thought Maxwell was all those wonderful things, well . . . the least he could do was try to be them, at least for a while.

Suddenly he saw exactly the log he was waiting for. It was wide enough to stand on and it had lots of branches to grab. And it was floating right toward him. "This looks like the one, Lester," he said, and stepped toward it. The water was now up to his chest. He reached out and grabbed the nearest branch and held on.

"Don't drop the old oil can, pal," exclaimed Lester.

"I won't," said Maxwell. He hung the oil can on a broken twig. "I'm going to need both hands," he said, and then he climbed up on the log and sat down. Lester was swinging from the twig. "Here we go," said Lester. "Just steer us to the middle of the dam, Captain!"

Maxwell began to paddle with his hands, moving the log into the center of the river. Abruptly, he felt a bump behind him, and the log tipped up in front. "Hey," he said, and looked around. It was Linda, soaking wet, climbing aboard. She shook, spraying water in all directions. "Linda," said Maxwell, "you were supposed to wait on the shore." Linda wagged her tail and sat down on the log, too.

"This is wonderful!" exclaimed Lester. "I've never been to sea before!" He was swinging from the twig, making *glop*-ing noises. "What a life!" he said. "Far from care and worry, from noise and people, from dark corners and oily rags. . . . Water on

every side, and the wind whistling—why, this is marvelous!" Lester began to sing—a high, happy sound. "Watch that big tree!" he shouted suddenly.

"I see it," said Maxwell. He paddled away from it, just missing a crash. "I like it out here, too," he said. "But it's scary."

"I'd like to float for miles and miles," said Lester. "See the world and all the wonders. . . ."

The dam was just ahead now. Maxwell aimed the tree toward the machinery that was sticking up.

"Get ready!" cried Maxwell. "We're going to bump!"

"Aye, aye, sir!" said Lester.

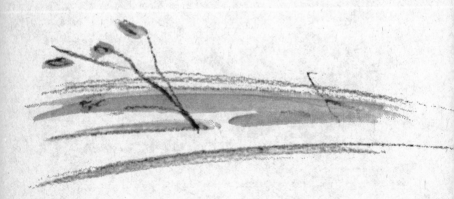

Maxwell reached out with one hand and took hold of the metal support. He held tight, even though it felt as if his arm might pull right out of his shoulder. The log turned slowly and stopped. Then Maxwell took Lester off the twig. "Where do you want to start, Lester?" he asked.

"Let me look it over," said Lester. "This will take a little study." There was a long silence, then Lester spoke. "Point me at that rusty crank there," he said. "That clearly needs some oil."

Maxwell put Lester's spout above the crank. *Glop-glop-glup-glop*. "There!" said Lester. "Now let's oil that chain—" *Glop-glup-glop-glop*.

Maxwell held tight to the metal and moved the oil can here and there as Lester instructed. Finally, it was done. "Hang me back on that twig, Maxwell," said Lester. "I've done all I can do. The rest is up to you."

"*Me*?" said Maxwell.

"You're the one with the muscle, Maxwell," said Lester. "Turn the crank if you can, and open the dam."

Maxwell held tight to the log with his knees and grabbed the handle with both hands. He tried to turn it. Nothing happened.

"Give it all you've got!" cried Lester, swinging from the twig.

Maxwell closed his eyes and took a deep breath. He could feel Lester and Linda watching him. He grabbed the handle again. "Now or never," he said aloud.

"You can do it, Max!" cried Lester.

13

The handle began to turn—slowly at first, then faster and faster, screeching. The chain moved upward, clanking by. "Hooray!" shouted Lester. "The dam is opening!"

Maxwell turned the crank as fast as he could. The door of the dam broke the surface of the water and rose up and up, until it was hanging in the air. With a roar, the water rushed through the opening. Branches and logs raced past, a torrent of water thundered by. Maxwell had to hold the support with both hands, so that the log would not go over the

waterfall. "Hang on, Max!" shouted Lester. "Hang on for dear life!"

Maxwell didn't think he could do it. His arms were aching now. But he knew that if he let go, they'd all be lost—Linda and Lester and himself. "I'll count to fifty," he said to himself. "I'll hang on till fifty, no matter what. . . ."

He could hear Linda barking, and the trees and branches bashing against the sides of the dam. "Nineteen . . . twenty. . . ."

"Just a little longer, Max!" called Lester.

"Twenty-six . . . twenty-seven. . . ." Maxwell felt the log bumping against something. He had to let go.

The log was thumping against the side of the dam. The water was getting lower and lower. Most of the dam was clear now, standing high and dry. Only a steady stream was going through the open part of the dam.

"You *did* it, Maxwell," said Lester. "Boy, are you strong!"

"*You* did it, Lester," said Maxwell. "You saved the town."

"It was a team effort," said Lester. "That's what it was."

Now the water was only about a foot deep, and Maxwell jumped off the log. "Are you okay, Linda?" he asked.

Linda wagged her tail and slid off the log, too. She paddled around in circles.

Maxwell jumped up and down in the shallow water. "Hot dog!" he shouted. He felt great.

Then he heard Lester calling from the twig. "Oh, Maxwell," he was saying. "Maxwell?"

Maxwell splashed over to the log. "Gee, I'm sorry, Lester," he said. "For a minute I forgot you were still hanging there." He lifted Lester off the twig.

"That's okay," said Lester. "I was tired anyway."

"You must be," said Maxwell. "All that oiling you did." He gave Lester a pat. "I'll get you back down to the village in a jiffy, Les."

"No," said Lester. "No, thanks."

"No?" said Maxwell. "You don't want to go back now?"

"Not now," said Lester. His voice was sort of strange and different. "Not now," he repeated, "or ever."

"What do you want to do?" asked Maxwell.

There was a pause. Then Lester said. "I think I want to float down the river."

"The river?" said Maxwell. "That could be dangerous, Lester."

"I'm pretty empty now," said Lester. "I think I'll float okay."

"But where will you go?" asked Maxwell.

"Wherever the river takes me," said Lester quietly.

"Listen, Lester," said Maxwell. "Why don't you come with Linda and me? We'll take you home to where we live. I've got plenty of things that need oiling all the time—a skateboard, and a jackknife if I can find it, and a lot of other stuff around the house. You'd like it there, and we could have a lot of fun."

"That's awfully nice of you, Maxwell," said Lester. "And if I wanted to live in any one particular place, I'd certainly want to live with you and Linda. You've been good friends to me, and I admire you both a lot."

"And we admire you, Lester," said Maxwell. "You're smarter than anybody in the third grade."

"Thanks, Maxwell," said Lester. "But I've made up my mind to go. I want to go down the river, wherever it goes. I want to see what there is to see."

"All by yourself?" asked Maxwell.

"I'm afraid so," said Lester. "I'd like you and Linda to come along, but you've got school to go to, and parents, and friends, and everything. Alone is the way it's going to be for me."

Maxwell didn't know what to say.

"Do me a favor, Maxwell," said Lester. "Take me over there to the opening in the dam, and drop me in the water. Okay?"

"If that's what you want, Lester," said Maxwell. He carried Lester to where the stream was moving through the opening in the dam. "We're going to miss you, Les," he said.

"Same here, Maxwell," said Lester. "It's been a pleasure to work with you."

"I hope you have a safe trip," said Maxwell.

"Thanks, Maxwell." Lester gave a couple of *glop*s. "Just launch me off, now," he said. Maxwell lowered the oil can to the water. Then he let go. The oil can bobbed away, then was caught in the current. "So long, friends!" called Lester, and then he was gone through the opening in the dam, moving down the river until he was out of sight.

14

Walking home, Maxwell barely had the strength to put one foot in front of the other. He and Linda trudged along the road, in and out of the puddles, and it seemed to take forever. But he only stopped to rest once. That was in front of the fire hydrant. "Harold?" he called. "Mr. Hydrant?"

There was no answer. The hydrant just sat there silently, as if it had never moved. Maxwell thought that maybe Harold felt badly about not being able to save the town. Maybe his pride was hurt. "Mr. Hydrant," Maxwell said, "I just wanted to thank you for all you did. Without you, I'd still be sitting

in the road and the town would be flooded. You did everything you could. You were great. So thank you, and good night."

Then Maxwell and Linda walked on down the road. When they were about twenty feet away, Maxwell thought he heard a low, rumbly voice behind him. It sounded like "You're welcome," but he couldn't be sure, and when he looked over his shoulder, the hydrant hadn't moved. It was just sitting in the shadows.

Pretty soon, Maxwell could see his house. His eyes were half closed, and he felt sleep coming over him. In his mind, though, he saw something moving. It was sort of shiny and bright, and it raced along. He knew what it was then: the small brown oil can, floating down the river, bobbing and dipping, turning this way and that, riding past the woods and the towns under open skies, all the way, perhaps, to an ocean far away, and then . . . . Maxwell was home.